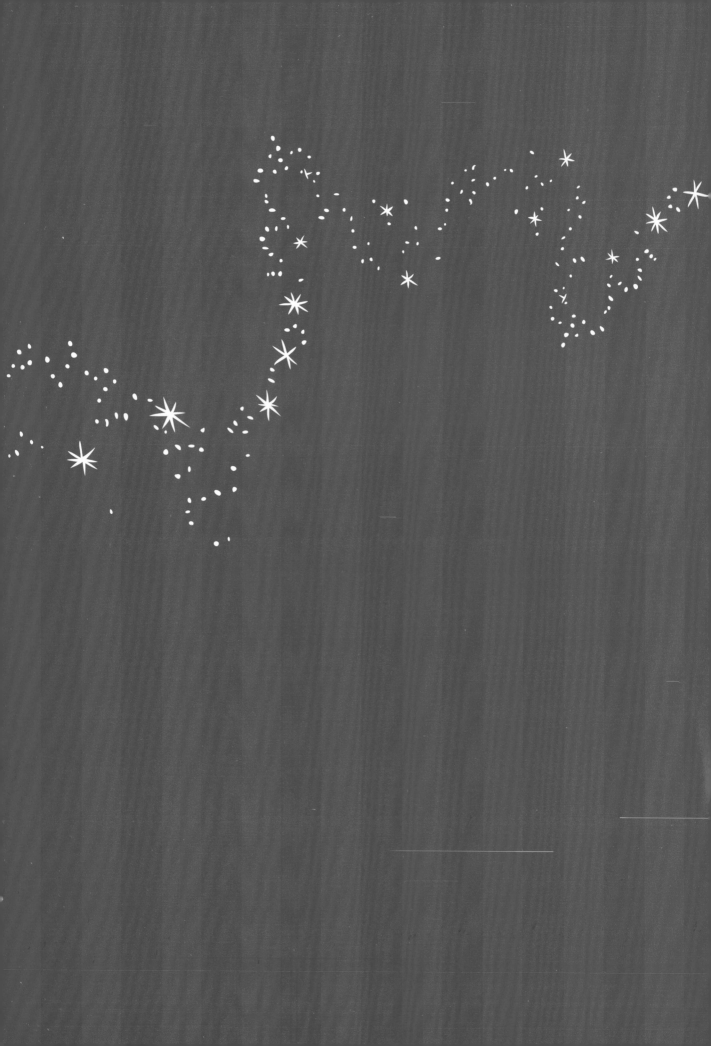

This book belongs to

_____

DISNEY

Mickey AND Friends

The Story of Mickey's Adventures

Disney

Mickey AND Friends

The Story of Mickey's Adventures

Bath · New York · Cologne · Melbourne · Delhi
Hong Kong · Shenzhen · Singapore

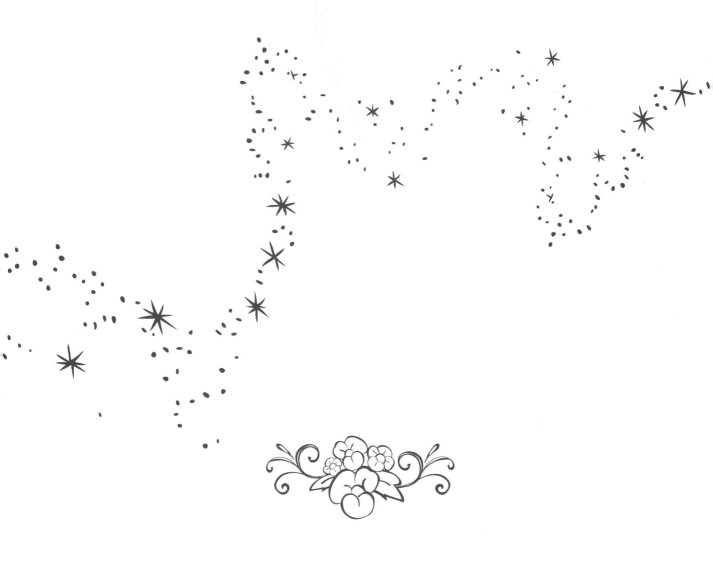

This edition published by Parragon Books Ltd in 2016
and distributed by

Parragon Inc.
440 Park Avenue South, 13th Floor
New York, NY 10016
www.parragon.com

ISBN 978-1-4748-5051-3

Printed in China

To laugh at yourself
is to love yourself.

Disney

Mickey AND Friends

A Perfect Picnic

It was a beautiful spring day. The sun was shining. The birds were singing. And Mickey Mouse was planning a picnic!

Suddenly, Mickey had an idea.

"Picnics are so much better with company,"
he told Pluto. "Maybe I should invite our friends to
join us. What do you think, boy?"
Pluto barked happily. He agreed with Mickey.

Mickey picked up the phone and called Goofy.
"Hiya, Goofy," he said. "How would you like
to have a picnic in the park? We can all make our
favorite foods, and then we can swap baskets!"

"Gosh, Mickey," said Goofy. "That sounds fun!
What should I bring?"

Goofy began to list his favorite sandwiches. "Cream cheese and marshmallow? Pickle and honey? Spaghetti and olive?" Suddenly Goofy shouted, "I've got it! I know just what to make. See you at the park, Mickey!" And with that, he hung up.

Mickey laughed as he put down the phone. Goofy sure did like some weird foods.

While Goofy made his lunch, Mickey invited his other friends to the picnic. First he went to see Minnie. "Oh, Mickey," Minnie said. "A picnic sounds like a perfect way to spend the day. And sharing all of our favorite foods sounds like so much fun. I can't wait!"

Mickey was on his way to Donald's house when
he ran into Donald and Daisy taking a walk.
"A picnic sounds like a wonderful idea," said Daisy.
"I know just what to bring!" said Donald.

Donald raced home and began to pack a lunch.
He took out two pieces of bread to make
a sandwich. He got out his favorite drink. Then
he chose a piece of fruit.

But as Donald looked at the food, he began to get hungry. *These are my favorite foods,* he thought. *I don't want to share them. I want to eat them myself!*

Over at Minnie's house, things were not going so
well either. Minnie had packed all of her favorite foods:
a peanut butter sandwich, lemonade, and an apple.

But as she got ready to leave, she started to wonder
if she would like the lunches her friends had packed.
I don't want to share my lunch with the others, she
thought. *I want to eat it myself!*

Daisy was excited about sharing her lunch. She hummed to herself as she packed her sandwich and drink. Then Daisy picked up a banana. . . .

Daisy thought about someone else eating her favorite fruit and began to frown. Maybe she didn't want to share her lunch after all. . . .

At Goofy's house, the kitchen was very messy!
Goofy was making lemonade to take to the picnic
by squeezing lots of lemons. He was soaking wet
and covered in lemon juice!

Goofy tasted his lemonade. It was delicious!
This is my best lemonade ever, Goofy thought.
I don't want to share it. I want to drink it all myself!

Mickey had finished packing his basket and was about to leave his house when Pluto began barking at him. Pluto grabbed Mickey's shorts and tugged.

Mickey followed Pluto into the kitchen. "Thanks for reminding me," he said, taking out a bone. "I wouldn't want to forget your lunch!"

Mickey didn't know that his friends had changed their minds. As he walked to the park, he grew more excited about the picnic.

Soon he was skipping and humming to himself. "Won't this be fun, Pluto?" he said. "I wonder what everyone packed for lunch."

When Mickey got to the park, he found his friends waiting for him. They all had baskets of food. But they didn't look very happy.

"What's wrong?" Mickey asked his friends.
"I don't want to share my lunch," Donald said.
"What if I don't like the lunch I get?" asked Minnie.
"Bananas are my favorite!" Daisy added.

Goofy nodded in agreement. Everyone wanted to eat their own favorite foods.

"Oh," Mickey said, disappointed. "I guess we don't *have* to share."

Minnie looked at Mickey. He looked so sad.
She didn't want to be the reason he was upset!
Minnie handed Mickey her picnic basket. "It's
okay, Mickey," she said. "I'll trade lunches with you."
"Really? Thanks, Minnie!" Mickey said.

Mickey's friends saw how happy Minnie had made Mickey. They wanted to make Mickey happy, too.

"Will someone trade lunches with me?" Donald asked, holding out his basket.

Daisy took Donald's lunch. Then she handed her basket to Goofy and he gave his basket to Donald.

Mickey laid out a blanket, and the friends got to work setting up their picnic.

Minnie passed out plates while Goofy handed out napkins. Daisy gave everyone a cup, and Donald set out forks.

Mickey opened his picnic basket first. When he saw what was inside, he started to laugh.

"What's so funny, Mickey?" Minnie asked. Then she looked in her basket and started to laugh, too.

Everyone had packed peanut butter sandwiches and lemonade!

The only difference in the baskets was the fruit.
Daisy had grapes.
Minnie had an orange.
Goofy had a banana.
Mickey had an apple.
And Donald had a pineapple!

"Isn't there some way we can
share our fruit?" asked Minnie.
"I have an idea," said Mickey.
"Leave it to me."

While his friends ate their sandwiches and drank their lemonade, Mickey cut up the fruit. He put it all in a bowl and mixed it together. Then he took the bowl back over to the blanket. He had made a big fruit salad!

"What a great idea," Minnie said as Mickey passed out the fruit salad.

"Now we can all try each other's favorite fruits!" Daisy added.

Donald nodded. "Thanks for inviting us, Mickey," he said.

As Mickey's friends ate their dessert, they realized that Mickey had been right. Sharing *was* fun, after all!

DISNEY

Mickey AND Friends

The Birthday Surprise

Mickey woke up and jumped out of bed. As he slipped his feet into his slippers, he said good morning to Pluto, just like he did every day.

Mickey ate his breakfast, like he did every day. He brushed his teeth, like he did every day. And he did his stretches, like he did every day. But today was not like every other day. . . .

Today was Mickey's birthday!

"What should we do today?"
Mickey asked Pluto.
But Pluto wasn't paying
attention to Mickey. He was
staring out the window.

Mickey looked out the
window, too. His friends were
walking past his house.
I wonder what they're doing,
Mickey thought.

Mickey looked closer. Donald was carrying cups and plates. Daisy was carrying lemonade. Goofy was carrying a bunch of balloons. And Minnie was carrying a big cake.

"Pluto!" Mickey shouted. "It looks like they're having a party!"

Mickey looked out the window again. "Do you think they know it's my birthday? Could they be having a birthday party . . . for me?"

"We'd better get dressed, Pluto," Mickey said. "Just in case!"

So Mickey dusted off his gloves and polished his buttons. He even brushed Pluto.

Soon, they were ready.

Mickey and Pluto sat in the living room and waited for their friends. They waited . . . and waited. But no one came.

Finally, the doorbell rang. Mickey jumped up
and raced to the door. He threw it open, ready for
his party. But there was no party outside. There
was only Donald. And he looked upset.

"What's wrong, Donald?" Mickey asked.

"My favorite hammock is broken," Donald told Mickey. "What am I going to do? I can't nap without it! Can you help me fix it?"

Mickey knew his friend needed his help. "Sure, Donald," he said. "Let's go!"

So Donald, Mickey, and Pluto set off to fix the hammock. As they walked, an idea popped into Mickey's head.

Maybe there is no broken hammock, he thought. *Maybe Donald is* really *taking me to my party!*

Mickey was so excited that he started to skip.

Donald led Mickey into his front yard.
He stopped in front of two trees and looked
down. There, on the ground, was Donald's
broken hammock.

Mickey looked around. There were no balloons and no cake. There was just one friend who needed his help. So Mickey helped Donald fix his hammock.

"That should do it," Mickey said as he finished tying the hammock's rope around a tree.

"Thanks, Mickey!" Donald said when the hammock was strung up between the trees again. Donald climbed into his hammock and was soon drifting off to sleep.

"You're welcome," Mickey said, confused, and he started to head home.

I guess there wasn't a party after all, Mickey
thought. Just then, he heard Minnie and Daisy
calling him. They wanted to show him something!
So Mickey went with Minnie and Daisy.
As he walked, Mickey began to wonder about a
party again.
Maybe they are taking me to my party! he thought.

Minnie and Daisy led Mickey to their flower garden.
"Ta-da!" said Daisy.
"Everything is blooming!" said Minnie.

Mickey looked around. The garden was full of flowers. And they *were* very pretty. But still, Mickey couldn't help feeling disappointed.

"Do you want to help us garden?" Minnie asked.

Mickey thought about it. He didn't have any other plans. So he helped water the flowers.

A few minutes later, Goofy ran up.

"Mickey! Mickey!" he shouted, tugging on his friend's arm. "You've got to see this. I've never seen anything like it!"

Mickey waved goodbye to Minnie and Daisy then rushed away with Goofy.

Goofy seems very excited, Mickey thought as his friend hurried him down the road. *I wonder what he wants to show me.*

Then Mickey realized Goofy must be taking him to his party!

Suddenly, Goofy stopped running.
"Look, Mickey," he said, pointing to a large rock.
Mickey looked all around, but there was no sign
of a party. Why was Goofy so excited?

Then Mickey looked down. Two snails were racing on the rock.

"Gosh! Watch 'em go!" Goofy said. "Have you ever seen anything so exciting?"

Mickey had never seen a snail race before. It was exciting, but not as exciting as a party!

Mickey and Pluto watched the snails race for a while. Then they headed home.

"Oh, well, Pluto," Mickey said. "I guess I was wrong. I guess there won't be a party after all."

Pluto whimpered. He had never seen Mickey look so sad.

Mickey hung his head low. How could everyone have forgotten his birthday?

Mickey walked up the path to his house. He opened the front door and stepped inside.

As he reached for the light switch. . . .

"Surprise!"

Mickey's friends jumped out at him.
They had planned a party after all. A
surprise party! For the first time all day,
Mickey had not expected it.

"I don't understand," he said. "I thought you were all busy today. How did you find time to plan a party . . . at my house . . . without me finding out?"

Minnie giggled. "We took turns keeping you busy," she explained.

"*Hyuck*," Goofy laughed. "You didn't even realize we were planning a party. I guess we're pretty sneaky!"

Mickey thought about his day. . . .
Donald's broken hammock.
Daisy and Minnie's flowers.
Goofy's snail race.
Now Mickey understood.

Mickey smiled a huge smile. He was glad his friends had tricked him. He loved surprise parties!

"Thanks, everyone," Mickey said, "for the best party ever! And the best birthday!"

Mickey's friends clapped and cheered, "Happy birthday, Mickey!"

DISNEP

Mickey AND Friends

A Summer Day

It was a hot summer day. Mickey Mouse and his friends were relaxing in his living room. The friends were just deciding what to do with their day, when *POP!* Mickey's air-conditioning broke!

"Maybe there will be a
breeze outside," said Minnie.
But there was no breeze.
Just nice, cool lemonade from
Mickey's refrigerator.

"What are we going to do now?"
asked Daisy.

Minnie looked around. "Hmmm. . ."
she said. "Maybe we could make fans.
Or we could try sitting in the shade
under the tree. . . ."

"Gosh! Those sprinklers look nice and cool!" said Goofy, pointing down at Mickey's lawn.

Donald nodded. "But there isn't enough water coming out of them to keep *us* cool!" he said.

As Minnie watched her friends looking at the sprinklers, she suddenly had an idea.

Minnie jumped out of her chair. "I've got it!" she shouted. "Let's go to the lake! There's always a breeze there, and there's so much to do!"

"What a great idea!" said Mickey.

"It *is* the perfect day for a swim," Daisy added.

So Mickey, Minnie, and their friends raced home to pack.

Everyone quickly threw their bathing suits and towels into a bag. Then they all headed back to Mickey's house.

In no time, the friends were on their way. They were so excited for their day at the lake!

"What should we do first?" Minnie asked.
Everyone had a different idea. Daisy wanted to
play basketball. Mickey and Pluto wanted to play
fetch. And Donald wanted to go fishing!

Before anyone could stop him, Donald raced off toward a little boat docked beside the water.

Donald was about to hop into the boat when Minnie called out to him. "Wait up, Donald," she said. "I don't think we can all fit in the boat. Let's do something together!"

"But the water looks so nice!" said Donald.

"Why don't we go for a swim?" said Minnie. "We can *all* do that!"

Donald wanted to go fishing, but finally he agreed. After all, they *had* come to the lake to go swimming.

The friends put away their toys and jumped into the water. . . .

"Aah," said Donald. "You were right, Minnie. This *was* a good idea!"

Minnie smiled to herself. She was glad she and her friends had found a way to cool off.

"I could stay in this water all day!" Daisy said.
And that is just what they did.

As the sun set and the day started to get cooler, Mickey, Minnie, and their friends got out of the water.

Mickey had a special treat for his friends. . . .

"Gee, guys," said Mickey as they
roasted marshmallows over a campfire,
"this really was the perfect day!"

Finally, it really *was* time to leave.
Mickey and his friends packed their
bags and got into the car.

"That was so much fun!" said
Donald as they drove home. "Let's
do it again tomorrow!"

Disney

Mickey AND Friends

The Kitten Sitters

"Guess what?" Mickey said to his nephews, Morty and Ferdie. "We're going to watch Minnie's kitten, Figaro, while she visits her cousin. Isn't that exciting?"

Before Morty and Ferdie could answer, Minnie
and Figaro arrived. Suddenly, the boys heard wild
clucking, flapping, and crowing coming from next
door, and Pluto came racing across the lawn. A big,
angry rooster followed close behind him.

"Pluto!" Minnie scolded. "Chasing chickens again! Aren't you ashamed?"

Pluto was a bit ashamed, but only because he had let the rooster bully him.

"It's a good thing Figaro is staying with you," Minnie told Mickey as she got into her car. "Maybe he can teach Pluto how to behave!"

Minnie was hardly out of sight when Figaro leaped out of Mickey's arms and scampered into the kitchen. With one quick hop, he jumped onto the table and knocked over a pitcher of cream.

Pluto growled at the kitten, but Mickey just cleaned up the mess.

"Take it easy, Pluto," he said. "Figaro is our guest."

At dinnertime, Pluto ate his food the way a
good dog should. But no matter how hard Mickey
and the boys tried, Figaro wouldn't touch the
special food Minnie had left for him.

At bedtime, Figaro would not use the cushion Minnie had brought for him. Instead, he got into bed with Ferdie and tickled his ears. Finally, he bounced off to the kitchen.

"Uncle Mickey," called Morty. "Did you remember to close the kitchen window?"

"Oh, no!" cried Mickey, jumping out of bed. The kitchen window was open, and Figaro was nowhere to be seen.

Mickey and the boys searched the entire house.
They looked upstairs and downstairs, under every
chair, and even in the yard. But they couldn't find
the little kitten anywhere.

"You two stay here," Mickey told his nephews.
"Pluto and I will find Figaro."

Mickey and Pluto went to Minnie's house first, but Figaro wasn't there. Next, they went to the park down the street.

"Have you seen a little black-and-white kitten?" Mickey asked a policeman.

"I certainly have!" answered the policeman. "He was teasing the ducks by the pond!"

Mickey and Pluto hurried to the pond.
Figaro wasn't there, but they did find some
small, muddy footprints.

Mickey and Pluto followed the trail of
footprints to Main Street, where they met a
dairy truck driver.

"Have you seen a kitten?" Mickey asked.

"I have!" cried the driver. "He knocked over my eggs!"

Mickey groaned as he paid for the broken eggs. Where was Figaro?

Mickey and Pluto searched the whole town, but there was no sign of the kitten. By the time they returned home, the sun was starting to rise.

Soon Minnie drove up. "Where is
Figaro?" she asked.

No one answered.

"Something has happened to
him!" Minnie cried. "Can't I trust you
to watch one sweet little kitten?"

Just then, there was a loud clucking from the yard next door. A dozen frantic hens came flapping over the fence, with Figaro close behind.

"There's your sweet little kitten!" exclaimed Mickey. "He ran away last night and teased the ducks in the park. Then he broke the eggs in the dairy truck and—"

"And now he's chasing chickens!" Minnie finished.

"I had hoped Figaro would teach Pluto some manners," Minnie said. "Instead, Pluto has been teaching him to misbehave! I'll never leave him here again."

"Pluto didn't do anything wrong," Ferdie said.

But Minnie wouldn't listen. She picked up Figaro and quickly drove away.

"Don't worry, boys," said Mickey. "We'll tell her the whole story later, when she's not so upset."

"Please don't tell her too soon," begged Morty.
"As long as Aunt Minnie thinks Pluto is a bad dog,
we won't have to kitten-sit Figaro."

Mickey smiled and said, "Maybe we should
wait a little while. We could all use some peace and
quiet." And with that, he and Pluto settled down
for a well-deserved nap.

The End